Teddy Bear Tales

Brown Watson
ENGLAND

Contents

Text by Maureen Spurgeon
Illustrated by Pamela Storey

© 1992 Brown Watson,
ENGLAND

Uncle Sailor Bill

Teddy is so excited today. His Uncle Sailor Bill has promised to take him and all his friends on a special boat trip to Plumtree Island, with a picnic and a sing-song around a camp-fire.

Only Mummy Bear seems worried. She has seen the big storm clouds gathering in the sky . . . .

Suddenly, down comes the rain.

"Quick!" cries Teddy. "Make for the boat-house!"

Poor Teddy! He and his friends have been looking forward to their special treat for so long – and now it looks as if it is all going to be spoilt.

"My Uncle Sailor Bill has sailed half-way round the world!" Teddy tells everyone. "A thunder storm won't stop him from getting here."

He has hardly finished speaking, when – guess who comes into the boat-house, shaking a shower of raindrops from his hat? That's right! It's Uncle Sailor Bill, smiling all over his face.

"Ahoy there, me hearties!" he calls out in his loud voice. "Just the weather for a shipwreck, eh?"

"A shipwreck?" echoes Teddy.

"That's right," smiles Uncle Sailor Bill. "Come on, shipmates! Let's collect up all the things we can use to keep afloat."

Then, do you know what Uncle Sailor Bill does next? He turns every chair upside-down!

"This is going to be the best shipwreck, ever," he keeps saying. "Teddy, see if you can roll up that mat, will you?"

"All right, Uncle," says Teddy.

Nobody quite knows what is happening, but it seems a lot of fun.

By the time they have finished, the boat-house looks such a mess! As well as the upturned chairs, there are planks of wood and empty chests all over the place, rolled-up mats and piles of old sacks . . .

Mummy Bear holds up her paws in horror – but Teddy and his friends are so busy enjoying themselves, they don't even think about the rain pouring down outside.

"Look lively, shipmates!" booms Uncle Sailor Bill. "Time to get all round the wreck without falling into the sea!"

"That means we must try not to step on the floor!" Teddy shouts out. "We don't want to get caught by the pirate king!"

"A pirate king?" Uncle Sailor Bill laughs. "First time I've ever been called that, Teddy!"

When they've all gone round the shipwreck at least twice, Uncle Sailor Bill calls out: "Time for ship's rations!" and throws back the lid of a great, big picnic hamper packed with all sorts of good things to eat and drink.

Then Uncle Sailor Bill takes out his concertina, and everyone is soon joining in with all the jolly songs that they know.

Suddenly, one of the little bears gives a cry.

"Look, everyone! It's stopped raining!"

"So it's a voyage to Plumtree Island, after all," says Uncle Sailor Bill. "Get the boat-house ship-shape, then we set sail."

The boat ride to Plumtree Island is lovely – but because of the rain, Uncle Sailor Bill says it's too wet to land.

"Sorry, shipmates," he says. "Maybe, next time, eh? When it's fair weather for sailing."

Teddy smiles round at his friends. Each of them can't help hoping for another shipwreck the next time they meet his Uncle Sailor Bill!

The Three Bears

Teddy Bear loves honey! Best of all, he likes it spread on hot toast at breakfast-time. So he's a bit disappointed when he sees Mummy Bear making porridge instead.

"Can't I have honey?" he asks,

"Porridge is good for you on cold mornings like this, Teddy," smiles Mummy. "Come and stir the oats with a little milk in my mixing bowl."

Mixing and stirring is usually one of Teddy's favourite jobs – but Daddy Bear notices that he doesn't look too happy about it, today . . .

"Don't worry about eating up your porridge," he smiles, sitting down in his big chair. "Someone might come along and start eating it for you."

Teddy stops stirring at once.

"Someone eating my porridge?" he cries. "I don't believe it!"

"I expect that's what the other three bears thought," says Mummy, pouring the rest of the milk into a saucepan.

"What other bears?" asks Teddy. He forgets about not having honey for breakfast. "Tell me, Mummy!"

"Well," says Mummy, "there was a Daddy Bear, a Mummy Bear and a Baby Bear. They lived in a cottage at the edge of a wood."

"Just like us!" Teddy says.

"Yes, that's right," Mummy nods, stirring busily.

"Well, this Mummy Bear had just made the porridge, but it was too hot. So, they went for a walk in the woods whilst it cooled down. And along came a little girl with such lovely, long, golden curls that she was called Goldilocks. She saw the three bears' cottage, and went inside."

"And did she eat the porridge?" asks Teddy.

"Only Baby Bear's! She tried Daddy Bear's porridge, but that was too hot, and she tried Mummy Bear's porridge, but that was too cold."

"Then what happened?" Teddy wants to hear the rest of the story, so Mummy tells him how Goldilocks sat in Daddy Bear's chair, but that was too hard.

"Then she sat in Mummy Bear's chair, but that was too soft."

"Did she sit in Baby Bear's chair?" asks Teddy.

Mummy nods again. "Yes. But she was so heavy after eating the porridge, she broke it in pieces! By the time the three bears came back, Goldilocks had gone upstairs to have a rest."

Teddy's Mummy has left the porridge on top of the stove to keep it hot. Now, when she pours it into the breakfast dishes, it is too hot to eat!

"Let's go for a walk," says Daddy. "Just down to the edge of the wood and back."

"Good idea!" agrees Mummy. "It's such a lovely, crisp morning. Put your scarf on, Teddy."

15

And as they go walking, Mummy finishes the story about Goldilocks and The Three Bears.

"But why did she go into the cottage when nobody was at home?" says Teddy at last.

"I think she smelt the porridge," says Mummy.

"And it was Baby Bear's porridge that she ate," Daddy reminds him.

"But, it's only a story. . ." begins Teddy.

16

Then, he stops. He is sure he has just seen someone going towards the little cottage at the edge of the wood . . . someone with long, golden curls bobbing about in the breeze . . .

"Come on!" he shouts, and begins to run as fast as he can. "Let's go home!"

He has quite decided that he doesn't want Goldilocks eating up **his** porridge, this morning!

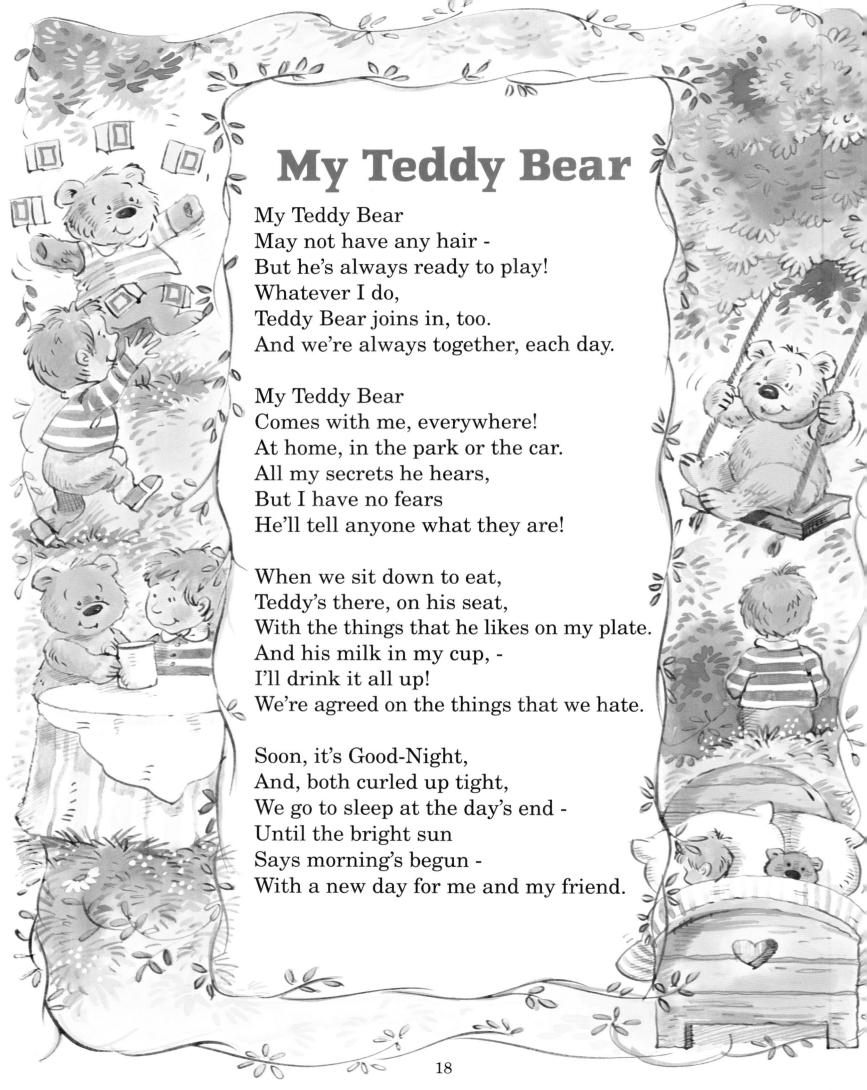

My Teddy Bear

My Teddy Bear
May not have any hair -
But he's always ready to play!
Whatever I do,
Teddy Bear joins in, too.
And we're always together, each day.

My Teddy Bear
Comes with me, everywhere!
At home, in the park or the car.
All my secrets he hears,
But I have no fears
He'll tell anyone what they are!

When we sit down to eat,
Teddy's there, on his seat,
With the things that he likes on my plate.
And his milk in my cup, -
I'll drink it all up!
We're agreed on the things that we hate.

Soon, it's Good-Night,
And, both curled up tight,
We go to sleep at the day's end -
Until the bright sun
Says morning's begun -
With a new day for me and my friend.

Grumpy Bertie Bear

Near the cottage where Teddy Bear lives with his Mummy and Daddy there are some lovely woods. He and Daddy Bear often go out walking and love to see all the birds and woodland friends.

"We've had a lot of rain lately," said Daddy one morning. "The ground's too wet to go far, Teddy, so I think . . ."

Teddy grabbed his Daddy's arm. "Listen!" he said. "I'm sure I heard a voice!"

"ATISHOO!" someone sneezed. "Oh, dear! Oh, dear! I feel so dreadful! And I ache all over!"

"Sounds like another bear!" cried Daddy, leading the way through the trees.

"Look, just under this clump of bushes."

"Who are you?" asked Teddy Bear kindly.

"The name's Bertie," answered the bear, sneezing again. "Ooh, I'm soaked to the skin!"

"You'd best come home with us," said Daddy Bear. "Take his arm, Teddy."

Before long, Bertie was sitting in Daddy's chair with Teddy's dressing gown on. And as he sipped a nice cup of hot chocolate, he began telling his story.

"I belong to a girl called Lavinia," he said.

He looked all around the cosy, little cottage.

"The house where we live is much bigger than this!" he added. Mummy Bear bit her lip.

"So, how did you come to be left in the woods?" asked Teddy politely.

"Lavinia went off picking flowers," growled Bertie. "I suppose she got caught in the rain and ran straight home. She would never have left me behind on purpose."

21

"No, of course not," smiled Daddy. "Look, we'll find you some dry clothes, then go back to the woods when you're feeling better, Bertie. Maybe Lavinia will be there looking for you."

Teddy managed to find a pair of trousers and a warm, woolly jumper to fit Bertie – even a pair of smart shoes and socks!

"Try these on for size, Bertie," he smiled.

Bertie Bear did not seem very pleased.

"Not really my colour," he said, fingering the jersey. "And Lavinia threw out a pair of trousers much better than these!" He gave a deep sigh. "Still, I suppose they are better than nothing. I'll get a whole set of new clothes once I'm back home, anyway."

"What a nasty, old bear," thought Teddy. "He hasn't even said "Thank You", yet!"

In the end, Mummy, Daddy and Teddy Bear were glad when the time came for Bertie to go back to the woods. Daddy and Teddy waited to see if the little girl would come back to find him. Presently, they heard a voice.

"Lavinia, dear, come here a minute!"

It was a little, old lady, squeezing her way towards the clump of bushes where Bertie sat.

"Lavinia," she smiled, as a little girl appeared, "isn't this the bear you lost the other day?" It was then that Teddy saw the lovely doll which Lavinia held.

"What, that old thing, Auntie?" she cried. "Look at him. Somebody must have thrown him away!"

Bertie looked as if he were about to cry. She went off, leaving the old lady to pick up Bertie Bear.

"Do you know," she said, stroking his head, "you remind me of a Teddy Bear I had when I was a girl, about the same age as my great niece, Lavinia. How would you like to come home with me? I'm sure my grandchildren would love to play with you when they come to tea."

The hurt look on Bertie Bear's face vanished in an instant.

Teddy could see the corners of his mouth turning up into a happy smile, his black eyes shining like new, just to know that he was loved and wanted once again.

"What are you thinking about, Teddy?" asked Daddy.

"I was just wondering," said Teddy, "if Bertie Bear will call at our cottage again."

Round and Round the Garden

Round and round the garden,
Like a teddy bear,
One step, Two steps,
Tickle you under there.

Round and round the haystack,
Went the little mouse.
One step, Two steps,
In his little house.

The Doll's House

Teddy Bear always likes calling in to see his friend, the Toymaker. His workshop is such a nice, warm place to be, with lots of interesting things going on.

"Nice to see you, Teddy!" the Toymaker smiled one morning. "Come over to my bench and tell me what you think of this doll's house I'm making for the Children's Hospital."

Teddy, thought how pleased the children would be.

"Isn't it their party tomorrow?" asked Teddy.

"Yes," said the Toymaker.

Next day, Teddy decided to go past the Children's Hospital on his way to the Toymaker's workshop.

Everyone was busy, putting up decorations and setting out the tables ready for the party.

"If only the children had something nice to see from their balcony, instead of this ugly, old wall," sighed Matron.

"Even the birds don't stay long because there is nowhere for them to feed!"

Teddy wished he could help.

"Not much fun sitting out on a balcony when there is nothing to see. Never mind!" he told himself. "Just wait until the Toymaker brings the lovely doll's house!" He could hardly wait to see it, himself!

But, as he turned the corner, the Toymaker came hurrying towards him, looking very upset.

"Such a dreadful thing has happened, Teddy!" he cried. "I left my workshop window open last night so that the paint would dry, and the rain came in and made the wood swell. Now the walls don't fit, so I can't put the floors in, either!"

"Oh, dear!" said Teddy. "And you worked so hard!"

Then Teddy had an idea!

"Toymaker," he said, "can you fix some hooks to the bottom of the house, and take out the back wall? Perhaps make the roof a bit thicker, too?"

"Yes," said the Toymaker in surprise, "but . . ."

"Do that, then bring it to the Children's Hospital," said Teddy. "I'll meet you there."

And off Teddy went into the woods with his Daddy. Together, they collected all the nuts and berries and pips they could find. Then Mummy Bear gave them some pieces of stale bread and an old saucer – and off they all went to meet the Toymaker at the Children's Hospital.

It really was a very good idea . . .

Soon, the Toymaker was fixing the strange-looking house on to the wall . . . And even before Teddy had put out all the berries, the nuts, the pips, the stale bread and a saucer of water, birds began flying in and out of their new home!

"What a sight for the children to see from the balcony!" cried Matron. "Thank you, Toymaker!"

"And thank you, Teddy!" smiled the Toymaker.